Stop!
Before you turn the page —
Take a piece of paper.
Pick up your pencil.
Draw a big triangle.

At the top point of the triangle, write **Secret Government UFO Test Base.** At the left point write, **Dinosaur Graveyard.** At the right point, **Humongous Horror Movie Studios.** And in the exact center of the triangle, write **Grover's Mill.**

Ah, Grover's Mill. A perfectly normal town, bustling with shops, gas stations, motels, restaurants, and schools. A small town with a great big heart, nestled snugly in the midst of —

Wait! Did we say *normal*? A studio where they film the cheapest horror movies ever made? The world's largest and smelliest graveyard of ancient dinosaur bones? A secret army base filled with captured alien spacecraft?

All this makes poor Grover's Mill the exact center of supreme intergalactic weirdness!

Turn the page.
If you dare.
Enter The Weird Zone!

There are more books about

THE WEIRD ZONE!

THE WEIRD ZONE

REVENGE OF THE TIKI MEN!

by Tony Abbott

Cover illustration by Broeck Steadman
Illustrated by Lori Savastano

A
LITTLE APPLE
PAPERBACK

ISBN 0-590-67440-4

12 11 10 9 8 7 6 5 4 3 2 1   7 8 9/9 0 1 2/0

Printed in the U.S.A.   40

First Scholastic printing, July 1997

To Helen, for all the laughs

Contents

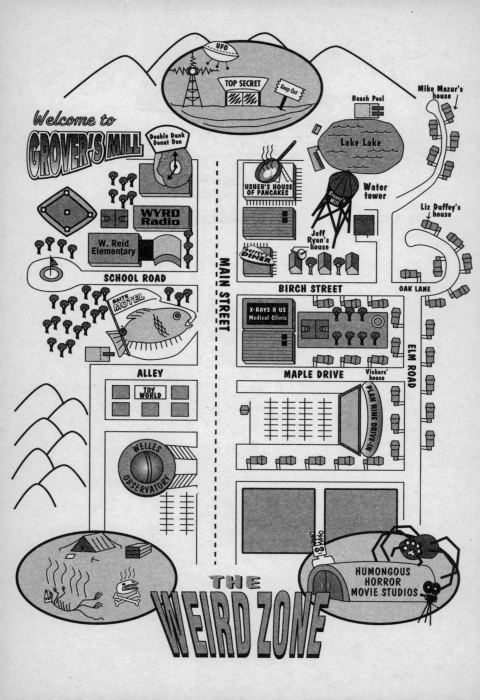

Non-Weirdness

Sitting alone on the top row of bleachers, Liz Duffey looked out over the baseball field behind W. Reid Elementary School.

"First day of summer vacation," she said to herself. "First Monday with no school. First baseball game. Incredible sunshine. This is all so — "

"Odd!" yelled a voice below her. "Odd-odd-odd!"

Liz frowned. "That's not what I was going to say . . . for once." She turned to see Mike Mazur and Holly Vickers standing behind home plate.

"I'm odd," Mike insisted, holding one

hand behind his back, ready to choose sides for the game.

"You're odd, all right, Mike," Holly said with a laugh. "So I guess I'll be even. Ready? Set. Go!" She thrust out her hand, showing three fingers.

Mike stuck out two fingers. "Ha! The odd team wins! I choose Liz and we're up first." He smiled up at Liz.

Liz made a face at him as she jumped down the bleacher steps to the field. "Oh, goody, I'm on the odd team. What I always wanted."

"Don't let it get you down, Liz," Holly joked. "Odd is pretty normal around here."

Holly's brother Sean strolled up to the plate with Jeff Ryan. "Odd, even. Why do we have to do math during the summer?"

Liz chuckled and handed a glove to Jeff.

"Baseball is the absolute coolest game," said Sean. He dropped a pair of bats and ground a brand-new baseball between his palms.

Bong! The Double Dunk Donut Den's

donut-shaped clock on Main Street chimed the hour.

Sssss! The pancake pan sitting high above Usher's House of Pancakes steamed the hour, too.

"And now it's official," Liz said, picking up one of Sean's bats. "Time to play ball!"

Holly pulled on a glove and took up her position at first base. Sean trotted to the pitcher's mound and began to stretch. Jeff strode out between second and third to his favorite position of shortstop.

"Blast one out to left field," Mike said, crouching behind the plate to catch for Liz. "You'll get a good triple at least."

Liz swung the bat around and nodded. "My dad told me that centuries ago this field had all kinds of caves running under it. Tunnels and pits and stuff that people used to live in."

Liz's father, Kramer Duffey, was an archaeologist who dug holes and found prehistoric fossils and artifacts all around Grover's Mill.

"Caves?" Mike mumbled. "That's weird."

From home plate Liz could see all the way north of town to the secret army base. Jeff Ryan's mother worked there. In the east was the Humongous Horror Movie Studios where Mr. Vickers made scary low-budget films. And in the west was one of her father's archaeological sites.

"Sure it's weird." Liz tapped the plate with the bat. "That's because Grover's Mill is right in the center of a giant triangle of weirdness. It's obviously been that way forever."

Mike laughed, pounding his glove with his fist. "At least since people used to live in those caves. Hey, wouldn't it be great if today turned out to be the first *non*-weird day? I mean, there's a first time for everything."

Liz tapped the plate again. She knew what he meant. Their town had had a lot of first times.

The first time zombie Martians attacked the earth was in Grover's Mill. The first

4

time a prehistoric dinosaur egg hatched out a living dinosaur was there. The first time octopus monsters from Planet X landed was there, too.

But the first non-weird day?

Tap! Tap! Liz tapped the plate again. The sounds echoed beneath her.

"Get ready to strike out!" Sean yelled, starting his windup.

Liz pounded the plate again, a little harder.

Boom! The ground rumbled deeply beneath the plate. It shuddered and quaked.

"Whoa! Did you hear that?" Liz said.

Mike stood up and frowned at the ground. "Sounds hollow . . ."

Liz pounded the plate some more. *Boom-boom-boom!* The ground around them started to shake and shift. Their legs wobbled as they tried to keep their balance.

"This isn't right." Mike threw down his glove and picked up the other bat. He started to pound the plate, too.

"Hey!" Jeff shouted. "One batter at a time."

But with every hit of the two bats, the ground rumbled and boomed louder and more deeply.

"Stop joking, you guys!" Sean yelled. "My fastball is gonna slow down if we don't start!"

"But — it's hollow under here!" Liz shouted.

RRRRR! The earth rumbled sharply. It swelled under the plate and shifted with a suddenness that caught Mike off balance.

"M-M-Mike, watch out! C-c-c-cave in!" Liz stammered. "The g-g-g-ground!"

The g-g-g-ground exploded!

KA-BOOOOM!

Home plate shot up like a rocket and the earth erupted from below with a loud *wumping* sound. Huge chunks of dirt and rocks blasted out everywhere.

The ground sunk beneath Mike suddenly and he tumbled into a deep dark hole.

"Help!" he screamed.

But he wasn't down there for long.

Something was coming up out of the ground.

Something very big.

2

Head's Up!

"**M**ike, what is going on?" Liz screamed, scrambling back to the backstop for protection.

"Something's down here! Something big! And it's moving!" he screamed from down below.

Dirt exploded out everywhere. The rumbling shook the earth under the field. Sean, Jeff, and Holly came running over.

A second later — *whoom!* — Mike rose up into view, sprawled on top of a giant flat stone. He leaped off when the stone came to the surface.

But the giant stone kept rising. It pushed itself up out of the ground and continued to blast up, higher and higher into the air. Ten feet. Twenty feet. Thirty feet!

It was big! It was huge! It was enormous!

Finally — *RMMMM!* — the stone stopped. The ground thundered once more, then fell silent. The dust cleared around the huge stone.

It towered over the field.

"Whoa!" Liz gasped when she saw the size of the stone. "That was *under* us? It's . . . it's . . ."

"It's humongous!" Mike cried, looking up from the ground. Then he squinted. "It's also carved like a statue."

Mike was right. The stone was a giant carved head. In the middle of the face was a long nose rising between sharp, high cheekbones. Underneath was a broad mouth and a jutting chin.

But those weren't the most striking features.

"Creepy!" muttered Holly, running over

to Liz and Mike. "The eyes. The eyes are so deep and creepy!"

"For once, I've got to agree with you," Sean said, moving up next to his sister. "Deep eyes are always creepy. Remember that movie our dad made? *The Creepy Creep with Eyes So Deep?*"

"Yeah, but that creep didn't show up to ruin a baseball game," Liz said. She looked up. Way up. "Talk about odd? How did this *thing* get here? And what even is it?"

Jeff jerked back from the big head. "Maybe he's . . . you-know-who. Grover."

"Grover?" Sean said. "Who's Grover?"

"You know, the original Grover of Grover's Mill?" Jeff said. "Maybe it's a statue of him."

Liz shook her head, circling around the big stone. "I don't think so. I've seen pictures of this kind of statue. But they're normally far away on jungle islands in the Pacific Ocean."

"Well, *normally* doesn't work around

here," Holly said. "Remember where we live?"

Liz made a face. "You've got a point." She stared at the big head.

Snap! Snap!

The kids turned and squinted into the sunlight. There they saw a man standing on the pitcher's mound, snapping his fingers.

"Who's he?" Holly whispered.

"And how did he get there without us seeing him?" Liz muttered. "Odd. Very odd . . ."

The man stepped down from the mound and danced lightly across the infield to them.

He was dressed in a bright turquoise suit with a velvet collar, narrow pants, and shiny black shoes. He wore sleek black sunglasses. "The big guy is what you call a Tiki man," he said. "Hey, that reminds me of a joke."

The man's hair was black, slicked flat on the sides, and combed to a high peak in

12

front. A curl dangled down to the middle of his forehead.

"What do you call a twenty-foot-tall Tiki man?" he said. The kids shook their heads.

"Shorty!" the man burst out. "Isn't that cool? And, hey, speaking of cool, so am I. Buddy Kool's the name. That's *Kool* with a capital *K*!"

"Uh-huh," said Mike, brushing the dirt from his pants. "Well, we were just trying to play a game and — "

"Watch the dust, kid!" the man said. "You want to uncurl my curl?" He pulled a small comb from his pocket and touched up his hair. "Am I perfect yet? Wait, don't answer. I already know I am!"

"Excuse me, sir?" Liz began, backing up into her friends. "But where exactly did you come from just now? I thought I saw — "

"Tssst!" the man hissed, putting a finger on his lips. "Buddy Kool talks, you listen. When Buddy Kool snaps his fingers, you listen, too."

"Listen to what?" asked Sean.

"This!" the man said. *Snap!*

Suddenly — *boom! boom!* The air echoed with booming sounds coming from the pitcher's mound. Liz glanced over to see five more strange shapes standing on the mound.

"More people!" she mumbled. "What's going on? How did *they* get here? And what are they wearing? They look sort of human, but . . . I don't know . . ."

The five figures hunched over to them. They did look sort of human — two arms, two legs, one head each — but they were completely covered in . . . weeds!

"Oh, you like the look?" Buddy Kool asked, peering over his sunglasses and brushing his fingernails on his jacket. "It's my great pleasure to introduce . . . the Mango Men. They've come to play!"

On their heads the Mango Men wore headdresses of shaggy, woven grass. Big floppy leaves crisscrossed their shoulders, and their pants were made of thick brown

twigs stuck together. They snapped and crackled when they walked.

But the strangest thing was the big, thick, ugly wooden stick that each carried.

"This is really starting to weird me out," said Holly.

"Okay, look, you want to play?" said Sean, walking up to the men, tossing a ball from hand to hand. "Some basic rules first. You guys have *way* too many bats — "

"Ugh!" one Mango Man grunted. He grabbed the ball from Sean, sniffed it, and took a bite.

Chomp! He began to chew it.

"Hey, that's a brand-new ball!" Sean whined.

"Hit it, men!" shouted Buddy Kool.

Boom! Boom! The Mango Men struck their big wooden sticks together. They snarled at the kids. They growled. They clacked their teeth like angry dogs.

Then they attacked.

Make Like a Tree — and Leave!

"**H**it it, Mango Men!" Buddy Kool repeated, jerking his fingers at the five kids.

In a flash the five wild Mango Men surrounded the kids and pushed them behind home plate.

"Don't hit anything!" Liz cried. "Especially not us!" She felt the wire backstop digging into her shoulders.

"We're trapped!" said Mike.

The Mango Men brought their sticks down suddenly and hit — the ground!

Boom! Ba-boom-boom! Ba-boom-boom! Ba!

"Oooh, so swingin'!" cooed Buddy Kool,

snapping his fingers to the beat. "Yeah! Make nice music for the people."

The Mango Men began to dance slowly around the giant head. They flapped their big floppy leaves like wings as Buddy Kool sang.

Tough to dance, in those crazy suits they wear.
Dressed like plants, insects living in their hair.
But they've come a long, long way.
Now they're here they're gonna stay.
It's not France, but, hey, your town's got flair!

"Faster with the pounding!" Buddy Kool urged his men. They pounded faster, and as they did —

Eeeee! The two deep dark eyes on the giant Tiki head began to glow. They glowed red! Then silver! Then green!

"Could this get any weirder?" Mike asked.

"Probably," Liz said. "What's happening with those eyeballs?"

Suddenly — *whoosh!* — a sharp breeze swept across the field. And the unbelievable happened.

The grass, so trim and neat, began to slither up through the ground in wild bunches!

In seconds, it was five, six, seven inches tall!

"Oh, man!" cried Sean. "There goes the field!"

"This is impossible!" Liz shrieked, watching the grass pour out under her feet. "It's incredible! It's like a videotape in fast-forward!"

"Ha-ha! More like fast-backward!" said Buddy Kool, chuckling mysteriously. "Right, my melodious Mango Men?"

"Ugh!" they agreed, pounding faster and louder. Then, as if calling to the kids from the real world, there were other sounds.

Bong! The donut clock chimed the hour.

Sssss! The pancake pan hissed it, too.

"Check, please!" Mike shouted, as dandelions swiftly coiled around his sneakers. "Me and my shoes are out of here!" He tore free of the winding weeds and ran.

Together the kids grabbed their bats and baseballs and tore off past W. Reid Elementary and down School Road away from the field.

"I think we can forget about this being a non-weird day, Mike!" Liz said, catching her breath.

"Right," Mike agreed. "Let's go tell your dad about the strange statues. It's archaeology. That's his department."

"It's also pretty weird," Holly added. "That makes it our department, too!"

But when they got to Main Street, the ground shook and quaked and rumbled again.

RRRRR! The street shifted from side to side.

"Oh, no! Not again!" cried Liz. Yes, again. A second giant Tiki man burst up from the ground at the north end of Main

Street. A third one exploded south of town at the movie studio. A fourth one shot up at the dinosaur graveyard in the west.

"Big heads are coming up everywhere!" cried Jeff.

"We're being invaded!" Mike shouted.

Then all the Tiki men's eyes glowed like the statue on the baseball field. They all seemed to be staring back at each other. Their eyes sparked.

Then — *ka-thoomp!* — a tall palm tree clustered with coconuts crashed through the sidewalk and wiggled up into the air. A dozen more followed it, swaying up and down the streets. Telephone poles sprouted giant leaves. Streetlights burst into bloom with wild, colorful flowers.

"Grover's Mill!" Liz cried. "The weird jungle thing is happening all over!"

And it was getting worse. With each rhythmic beat of the Mango Men's sticks on the ground, the town was becoming more and more jungly.

Boom! Big leafy plants exploded from

all the mailboxes. *Boom!* The benches on Main Street became masses of tangly vines. *Boom!* Wild branches blasted out the front windows of the supermarket, Pay & G'way.

"Down! You bad greens!" gasped Sean, swinging his bat below him as he leaped over a sewer grate with long green tendrils swirling out.

"We need lawn mowers just to walk down the street!" Jeff cried.

Boom-boom-ba-boom! The pounding went on.

"It's Buddy Kool and his Mango Men," said Mike, squishing a bunch of unruly flowers. "I think they're making this happen."

"Let's go to my house right now!" Liz called out. "We'll be safe there and we can call my dad. He'll know about these giant Tiki heads. Come on, it's our only chance!"

Liz scrambled up a hedge of vines, jumped down the other side, and headed for Oak Lane. A few minutes later, she and

her friends batted their bats through a dense wall of thickets.

"I think I see your house," Mike said, cautiously. "Well, I think it's your house. It's hard to tell."

Liz peered over the mass of green growth that half hid her street. Her heart sank. Yes, the yellow shape ahead of them was her house. But it was different now.

Giant vines twirled out of the flower border near the lamppost. The driveway was full of holes where tall weeds had already broken through. A lush tree poked through the porch.

It was a mess. But it was her house.

"Follow me!" she yelled. She ran as fast as she could and rushed for the front door just as a giant vine coiled up the steps toward the knob.

"Yuck!" muttered Jeff. "This vine's all slimy!"

Liz tried to jump away, but it grabbed her ankle. "Let go!" she cried, kicking her foot wildly.

"Off my friend, you dumb weed, or I'll prune you!" Holly shrieked, trying to pull Liz free.

But the vine was strong. It tugged Liz down the steps. It pulled hard, as if it had muscles. As if it could think. As if all of its thoughts were bad!

Liz clung to the railing, but lost her balance. "Help!" She stumbled back down the steps.

Instantly, the vine's long green fingers coiled thickly around her arms.

They had her tight in their grasp.

They pulled her swiftly to the ground.

Head for Home!

WHACK-WHACK! Mike swatted the vine again and again with his bat. "Back off, you stinky weed! You're not getting Liz!"

Sean and Jeff stomped on the vine while Holly tried to peel its slimy fingers off Liz's arms.

"Let her go!" they screamed as they struggled.

Thlurppp! The vine loosened its grip for a fraction of a second and Liz's friends pulled her quickly through the door.

WHAM! Mike slammed it shut.

Liz slumped to the floor, out of breath. "Thanks, guys! Nature is sure zoning on us today!"

"Yeah, your lawn's got a definite attitude," Sean said, peering back out the window.

Mike stood next to him and watched. In seconds, slithery plants crawled up the side of the house and covered the door. "This is pretty much the craziest thing I've ever seen."

"My shoes are all messed up," said Jeff, scraping green slime off his sneakers on the doormat.

"It's those giant Tiki heads," Liz groaned, double-locking the door behind them. "They're doing something very strange here. I don't know what, exactly, but it has something to do with those eyeballs and those Mango Men and that . . . that . . . uncool Buddy Kool! Guys, we're definitely on a weird alert."

Mike turned and caught a glimpse of something in Liz's living room. "Uh, then you probably won't like what's been happening here," he said softly. "Unless you, uh, like green a lot."

Liz held her breath. "It's not my favorite color." She turned around slowly. "Oh, no!"

Spiky plants were sprouting wildly from the corners of the living room. The piano at the far end was overgrown with grass, as if it had green fur on it. The sofa was prickly with thorns, and bark was growing over the cushions.

"No place to relax here," Sean said.

"Total jungle," said Jeff.

Beneath their feet the rug was sprouting puffy toadstools. Moss crept slowly down the walls.

Liz gulped. "My mom is going to have a fit! She hates green as much as I do."

Thlurppp! The television was up near the ceiling, in the grip of a giant plant. Making its way down the trunk was a long thick snake.

Mike gulped loudly. "I don't like snakes." He stepped back to the front door. "I really don't."

Liz glared at him. "*You* don't like snakes? You think *I* like snakes? I hate

snakes. Especially snakes in my own house!"

"Okay, okay, everybody," said Holly. "How about we move to another room?" She stepped into the kitchen. Something green unfurled from the sink and looked at her. "Nope, not that way. I think up is the way to go."

"Definitely," Jeff said, tearing his feet away from a snarly clump of grass and heading for the stairs. "While we can still move."

"Those things really seem to like you, Jeff," said Sean.

Liz gulped, rubbing her arms where the vine had clutched her. "Let's just hurry. I don't want to shake hands with any more green slimy things."

BRNNNNG!

"The phone!" Liz cried. "Yes! It might be my dad!"

They rushed up the stairs and scrambled into Liz's bedroom only to find the walls covered with flowers. But it wasn't Liz's wallpaper.

"The house is alive!" Mike said, watching tiny green tendrils stretch out from an electrical socket in the wall.

BRNNNNG!

"Quick," yelled Liz. "Before they hang up!"

Sean searched the bushes growing around Liz's night table. "I don't see the phone! There's a clock, and a book, and a box of tissues, and — "

BRNNNNG!

"We've got to find it!"

Liz leaped over to the top drawer of her desk and pulled out a purple plastic ruler. She dived at the thick bushes. She sliced at the vines. She chopped at the weeds. *Chop! Chop!*

BRRR — "Got it!" Liz yanked the phone up.

"Liz," said the voice. "This is your father. I — "

"Dad!" Liz screamed into the phone. "The jungle is all over our house, and — "

RRRRR! Rumbling and quaking shook the house suddenly, throwing the kids to the floor! Terrible crunching noises echoed up from the basement.

"Oh, no! Not again! Another Tiki man!" Liz screamed into the phone. "Dad! Another Tiki man is coming up from our basement!"

"Let's get out of here!" called Holly.

KRRAKK! The living room floor shattered as the giant head crashed up from the basement.

"Before it's too late!" Mike pushed open Liz's window and kicked out the screen. A big, shaggy tree was growing right outside. Long vines curled around on it, reaching for the house.

"Everybody out!" Sean yelled. He climbed out the window to the nearest limb. Holly followed him, then Jeff.

RRRR! The stone head pushed into the

living room below, throwing couches and end tables out of the way.

"Dad!" cried Liz. "We've got to get out!"

"Get to the museum right away!" her father yelled into the phone. "We've found the answer to the — "

Nnnnnn!

"The phone's dead!" said Liz.

"Let's not be next!" said Mike, half out the window and holding his hand out to Liz. "Will you come on!"

Liz took one more look around her room and jumped to the window just in time.

KA — KROOOOM! The fifth giant Tiki head exploded up through the floor.

Liz and Mike swung out to the tree and followed their friends to the ground just as —

KRUNCH! The giant stone Tiki man burst from the roof and rose up over the house, sending splinters flying in all directions.

The kids scrambled across the yard and back out to the road. Liz felt angry when she saw the damage to her house. She gritted her teeth. "Somebody's going to pay for this."

Boom! Ba-boom-boom! Mango Men emerged from the thickening jungle and circled the new stone head. They pounded

34

the ground. They flapped their floppy leaves.

A moment later, Buddy Kool was there, too, snapping his fingers.

"Wherever that guy is, something bad happens," whispered Holly.

Sean gripped his bat. "Yeah, I wish we could take these guys on right now. We'd break their branches. We'd rake their leaves."

Eeeee! As the pounding got faster, the eyes on the big head began to glow. Soon Liz's house was completely overgrown with thick gooey vines. The vines spread to the sidewalk and across the road.

Mike motioned to his friends. "Come on, let's get to the museum. Between my parents and Liz's dad, we'll get to the bottom of this." With his bat held high, Mike started bashing his way into the jungle. The others followed.

Looking up one last time at the giant Tiki man sticking out of her roof, Liz wasn't so sure science would help. Who knew if there even was a bottom to all this? Maybe the whole thing was . . . bottomless!

Like one of those caves under Grover's Mill.

Like one of those deep dark pits!

After battling their way for what seemed like forever, the five friends finally saw the dome of the Welles Observatory and Science Museum.

"There it is!" cried Mike, clobbering a tough weed that lay in his path. "The place where science rules."

Rrrrr! The ground rumbled under them again.

"Hurry," Liz urged. "It's getting worse." The kids tore up the broad steps, through the massive double doors, and into the museum.

Inside the large rooms it was almost normal. The jungle was climbing up outside the double-paned windows, darkening them. But it hadn't broken through the thick stone walls. Yet.

"The laboratory is straight ahead in the big room," Mike said. "It's where all the research and stuff happens. Where they find the answers to scientific questions."

"That sure sounds good," said Liz, rushing ahead. "Answers to questions. Because I sure have lots of questions."

But when the kids entered the vast laboratory, things didn't look good.

The first thing they saw was Mr. and Mrs. Mazur scribbling lots of words all over a large chalkboard. Actually, they were scribbling one word lots of times.

The word was — *Help!*

"Uh-oh," Liz said, turning to Mike and making a face. "Something tells me your parents are still working on the answers."

Mr. and Mrs. Mazur waved cheerfully and kept scribbling. Behind them — *nnnng!* — a huge complicated piece of machinery was whirring and chugging in a back corner of the laboratory.

Next to the machine stood Liz's father, Kramer Duffey. He was dressed in a leather jacket and field pants. A bullwhip hung on his belt, and a length of rope was coiled on his shoulder.

"Cool!" Mike whispered. "His outfit is so great."

Liz ran over. "Dad, giant Tiki heads are coming up everywhere! And there's a weird guy named Buddy Kool — "

"With a K!" Mike added. "He's doing weird stuff, and whenever he snaps his fingers — "

"These guys dressed like walking plants start to pound their huge sticks — " added Holly.

"They're called Mango Men," Jeff cut in, "and they dance and flap these big floppy leaves — "

"And then the Tiki men's weird eyes go real bright and silver," said Sean, "and that's when the jungle happens and — "

Mr. Duffey looked from Liz to Mike to Holly to Jeff to Sean and back again while he listened. When they were done, he shook his head slowly in silence. He looked over at Mr. and Mrs. Mazur, who had stopped writing on the board.

"It's exactly like the old legend!" he said.

Mr. Mazur nodded and pushed his glasses up his nose. "Actually, yes." He rolled a nib of chalk between his fingers. "Quite strange, too, this jungle effect. For, in fact, Grover's Mill was a dense tropical jungle centuries ago."

"Centuries ago," said Mr. Duffey. "That's the past."

"At that time," Mrs. Mazur continued, "the town was completely surrounded by water. All that's left of that ocean is Lake Lake."

Liz stood there, stunned. She narrowed her eyes. "Uh . . . the old legend? What old legend?"

"Oh, you know," said her father. "The one that says that giant Tiki men would pop up everywhere one day and make our town a jungle."

"No," said Liz. "No, I didn't know."

Mr. Duffey looked shocked. He turned

to Mr. and Mrs. Mazur. They shrugged. "Oops!" Mr. Duffey said. "I guess we forgot to tell you kids. But no one ever thought it would really happen! I mean, wouldn't that be just a little *weird*?"

Ching! The big machine suddenly stopped making noises and spat out a little strip of paper. "Ah!" said Mr. Duffey, his face brightening.

"But the Tiki men will go away, right?" asked Mike.

His parents shrugged. "Sorry, son," his mother said. "We can't remember that part."

Liz started to pace the giant room. "Let me get this straight. We don't really know why the Tiki men came up from under the ground?"

"That's right," Mr. Duffey nodded.

"But we have to stop them?" Liz said.

"That's the easy part!" he replied. "And all because of this!" Mr. Duffey held up the little strip of paper that had come from the big machine.

Mike frowned at the paper. "What do we do, fold it really tight and hit them with it?"

Mr. Duffey shook his head. "No, that wouldn't work. Using this big fancy device we have located the famous *Tiki Key*, the ancient stone tablet with all the answers! It'll tell us everything we need to know to stop these big old stone heads."

Liz looked at the sheet of paper her father held. "And where is this incredible Tiki Key?"

"Actually, that is where science steps in." Mr. Mazur flipped over the chalkboard to reveal a map of Grover's Mill. He took the paper from Liz's father and drew an X on the map.

"I knew it," Liz gasped. "The baseball field!"

"It's buried in one of the caves under the field," Mr. Duffey said. "All we have to do is leave here, hack through the jungle, get to the ball field, find the right hole, climb in, dig up the stone, bring it up, dust it off,

read what it says, translate it, do what it says, and the Tiki men should be a thing of the past."

"That's all, huh?" Liz muttered.

"Actually, the Tiki men *are* a thing of the past, ha, ha," Mr. Mazur said. "That's a little, ah, science joke."

"But you're sure this will work?" Mike asked.

Mr. Duffey shrugged. "If it doesn't, it's the end of civilization as we know it."

Thurrrlp! All of a sudden, they could hear vines and shrubs and trees slithering up the sides of the building.

"The jungle is getting closer!" Jeff said. "The vines are all around us!"

KA — RRRRUNCH!

Instantly, the massive double doors of the museum burst into splinters!

And the jungle poured in!

The Deep Dark Pit

THURRRLP! The jungle took over the laboratory in an instant. Long slithery vines barreled across the floor, instantly trapping Mr. Duffey and Mr. and Mrs. Mazur against the back wall. "Ouch!" they cried.

"Dad!" Liz cried out, running to her father.

"No! You kids get out of here," he yelled back. "Find the you-know-what and stop the you-know-who! Here!" He threw his climbing rope to Mike. "Save our town!"

"Come on!" Liz called to her friends. "We're the only hope!"

But Jeff and Sean bumped into each

44

other, trying to be first to the back door.

"Ooof! Some hope we are!" Jeff muttered, as thick vines quickly swirled around him and pinned him against the chalkboard next to Sean.

Holly dived past, but a giant flower closed on her legs, holding her down. "Holy Zabajaba!" she cried. "This is crazy!"

Within seconds they were all trapped.

"Save yourselves!" Sean yelled bravely to Mike and Liz, swinging his bat. "But if you don't come back for us, we'll never play baseball with you again! Now go!"

Liz looked at Mike. Mike looked at Liz. There didn't seem to be any choice.

"We're out of here!" Mike said, pulling Liz by the arm and slipping out the back door. "But we'll be back, you can count on it!"

"Please, no more math!" Sean mumbled.

Liz and Mike skittered along a narrow hallway and out the rear door of the museum into the thickening jungle. They ran for a long time.

"Wait up," Mike murmured, slowing to catch his breath. "I think we're lost."

"We're not lost," Liz snorted, looking into the dense greenery and trying to feel brave. "I just don't know where we are."

Mike gave her a look. "Isn't that the same — "

"Shhh!" she hissed. "I hear something."

Mike crouched next to her. "Pounding?"

"No," Liz whispered, "singing."

With a little grass shack for an office,
And a bamboo desk for two,
We could learn what goofing off is
Like, just me and you.

Liz pulled aside a thick wall of vines and peeked through. "It's . . . Mr. Bell! Uh, hello, sir!"

Mr. Leonard Bell, principal of W. Reid Elementary School, always wore a suit. Now he was dressed in a grass suit, with a grass necklace around his neck. Assistant principal Miss Lieberman was dressed the same. They were pushing their way through the thick jungle.

"Ahem! Children!" boomed the principal, resting his hands on his hips. "Have either of you two young students seen my house?"

"What color is it, sir?" asked Liz, trying to be helpful.

"Green," the principal answered.

Mike looked at Liz, then beyond her at the thick green growth all around. "Sorry, tough color. But can you tell us where school is from here?"

"We need to get there fast," Liz added.

Mr. Bell brightened. "Ah, excellent. Good to see your enthusiasm for your school. It is, after all, only another seventy-two and one-quarter days until we reopen."

"Our school is one-eighth of a mile in that direction," said Miss Lieberman, pointing up ahead. "Between the twelve-and-a-half-foot waterfall and the one-third-acre alligator swamp."

The principal beamed. "Ah, the wonder of fractions! A summer math program would be a splendid way to spend the summer, hmm? Well, let us go, Miss Lieberman. Much to do!"

In a moment Principal Bell and Miss Lieberman were gone.

"Our school is between a waterfall and a swamp?" Liz breathed. "Mike, this is really getting me down."

They pushed on, right into a crowd of shouting people.

"My husband is stuck in those branches!" screamed one woman, rushing through the trees. She pointed up to a man wearing a barbecue apron. "And he's so afraid of heights!"

"Put me down!" the man screamed. He swatted a long vine with a burger spatula.

"I found my car," cried another man, jingling his keys wildly. "But where's my garage?"

"Why must I have Tiki men in my town?" shrieked Mr. Sweeney, the janitor of W. Reid Elementary.

A moment later the crowd rushed by and the jungle grew quiet once again.

"Come on," Mike said. "We're not far now."

They were out of breath when they finally reached the school baseball field.

The field was totally overgrown and full of open pits and caves. The giant Tiki man stood tall and silent over what used to be home plate.

"It's like some weird jungle adventure movie," Mike said, breathing hard.

"Except that you can leave a movie." Liz sighed. "I don't know if we'll ever get out of this one, Mike. I mean, the way things are going, this could be our last adventure."

"Never say that!" Mike looked at her. "It'll take more than big stone heads and guys with sticks to stop us. Even though I have to admit this is pretty much the strangest day I've had for a long time."

"Yeah. Non-weird, it's definitely not." Liz cracked a smile as she pulled out the strip

of paper the machine at the lab had spat out. She stepped over to a hole near third base. It was dark. Liz couldn't see the bottom, but she felt as if the pit was calling to her. "Mike, I think this is where the Tiki Key is buried."

"What if we can't read the message?" Mike said.

"Well, we have to try," Liz said. Looking down into the pit, her head felt light. Her stomach did flips. The deep dark pit was very deep and very dark.

"You know how I hate deep dark holes," she reminded Mike. "And I really don't want to get stuck down there. But having your town turn into a jungle is beyond weird. We have to stop all this craziness."

"Before it stops us," Mike said as he uncoiled her father's rope.

Liz tied one end around her waist. "My dad says archaeology is a science that helps you keep both feet firmly on the ground!"

Liz's two feet left the ground as Mike

lowered her into the pit. She swallowed
hard.

Errrk! She dangled lower and lower on
the rope.

The pit got narrower as she descended.
Her elbows scraped the sides.

"I really really hate this!" Liz yelled.

Trapped, Captured, Caught!

"The things I do for my town!" Liz shouted up to Mike. Finally, she reached the bottom of the pit and started to scrape around in the dirt.

Tap-tap! "Hey, there *is* something here. Something flat and smooth." Liz scraped some more.

"The Tiki Key?" asked Mike. "Does it tell us what to do?"

"I don't know yet," Liz yelled back. "Wait, yes. It's got markings all over it. I've got it! Hoist me up!"

"We're saved!" cried Mike, as he quickly pulled Liz back to the surface. "Yahoo!"

At the top of the pit, Liz dusted herself

and Mike dusted the strange flat stone.

"Wait a minute, you can't read any of this stuff," Mike complained. "It's just a bunch of wavy lines."

Liz examined the stone then flipped it over. "Maybe this picture will give us a clue. A big triangle shape with a spiral over it. What could it mean?"

"Hey, your dad's the archaeologist," Mike said, crouching next to her.

Liz traced the lines on the stone. "It looks like a map. This line goes from the ball field to the top of Main Street. And then it goes to my house. Exactly where the Tiki men have been popping up. They're making a triangle around the town."

"But what do they want?" Mike asked.

Liz was quiet for a moment. "They want Grover's Mill! They want it like it used to be. The past, the jungle, everything. They want it back!"

Mike thought about it. "So it's true. When the Mango Maniacs pound the ground with their sticks and do their crazy dance, the Tiki men pop up."

Liz nodded. "Remember how I pounded home plate this morning? That's what started all this. It's like some kind of ancient knock-knock."

"Only not so funny," Mike said.

"Right," Liz said, looking at the stone again. "And the Tiki men have weird ancient powers in their eyes that can turn things back into a jungle. Back to the way they were centuries ago."

"That's the past," Mike said with a smile.

Liz nodded. "They made the jungle come back. Why? Because they want to live here again."

Mike was silent as he took in what Liz said.

She, too, wondered what it meant to go back to the beginning of time. A total jungle world. Green everywhere. Her least favorite color. She turned the stone over. "We need to find out what these words mean. Maybe we can bring our town back to normal, I mean . . . well, you know what I mean."

"The way it was yesterday. Yeah, I like that idea," Mike admitted. Then he frowned. "But one thing I don't get. Where does Buddy Kool — "

"Shh!" Liz hissed. "I think I hear something."

Twigs snapped behind them. Leaves crackled and whooshed. Sticks thumped and clacked. The sounds were getting closer.

"Mango Men!" Mike gasped. "They found us!" The two kids began to run as quickly as they could, scrambling away from third base. Mike held the Tiki Key under his arm. Liz hurried after him.

Boom-ba-boom! But the Mango Men weren't far behind.

"Keep going!" Liz yelled, jumping ahead of Mike. "And watch out for *h-h-h-holesssss!*"

As she said this, Liz leaped over a gnarly stump. When she came down on the far side, the ground wasn't where she thought it would be.

"Helllllp!" Liz cried as she tumbled — *wump!* — into another deep dark pit.

"Helllllp!" cried Mike as he tumbled after her — *wump!* — into the same deep dark pit.

"Ugh!" said the Mango Men as they quickly surrounded the pit and looked into it. They clacked their sticks and did a little dance.

"Oooh! What do we have here?" It was Buddy Kool. He leaned over the hole and looked down at Liz and Mike. His slick sunglasses glinted. So did his slick hair. "Didn't you know this whole area is full of pits? Looks like you fell for this one. Get it? Fell?" He chuckled.

"You!" Liz snarled under her breath. "We know what you're doing. You and your Mango Men and your big giant heads are trying to turn back the clock!"

"Yeah," said Mike, moving forward. "Well, we're going to yank out that clock's

batteries! With this!" He held up the Tiki Key.

"Oh! Thanks for finding that!" said Buddy Kool. "Seriously, we've been looking all over!" In one swift move he reached down and grabbed the stone tablet from Mike.

Liz glared at Buddy Kool. "You'll never get away with this!"

The man smiled. "I wonder if you'll talk so tough from inside a sharkskin suit. A living shark, that is!"

"Ugh!" the Mango Men grunted. A moment later, the kids were hoisted out of the pit and being pushed through the vines to the pitcher's mound.

"I love this," Liz mumbled. "Captured by a bunch of men in very scratchy grass suits."

"With big sticks," Mike added.

"Who grunt a lot," said Liz.

"Ugh! Ugh!"

Caw! Caw! Grrrr! Yap! Yap! Woo-ooo!

Strange animal calls and growls filled the air as the Mango Men pushed Liz and Mike down a hole at the pitcher's mound.

At the bottom of the hole was a bamboo door.

When the door swung open, Liz gasped. "There's a whole world down here!"

"I call it the Junga-Lounge," said Buddy Kool.

"Ugh!" said a Mango Man, prodding the two kids across a rope bridge swinging between some trees. A pool below the bridge swished.

Sloosh! The giant head of a large white

shark pierced the water's surface. Its beady eyes shot dark looks up at the kids.

Snap! The shark snapped its jaws loudly, bumped the bottom of the bridge with its nose, and dived.

"I'll count my toes later," said Mike. "Can we please just get off this bridge?"

The Mango Men moved the kids onto a winding stone path.

Slishhh! A hissing, steaming waterfall roared down one wall.

"Incredible," Mike gasped, nudging Liz. "It's just like a theme restaurant."

Liz saw an alligator slithering behind the waterfall. "But I wonder what the theme really is."

A moment later, they entered a clearing surrounded by blazing torches. In the middle were tables shaped like big flat mushrooms.

The Mango Men pushed Liz and Mike down at a table. Clusters of coconuts clung to a short palm tree that poked up through the table.

On the table were juice drinks with little paper umbrellas sticking out. Next to them was a straw basket heaped with curly french fries.

Mike reached for the basket. "I am so hungry!"

"Mike!" Liz slammed his hand down. The curly fries instantly uncurled and slithered across the tabletop and up the tree. "I think those fries need another couple of minutes!"

"Uh . . . thanks," Mike mumbled.

Boom-boom-ba-boom! The Mango Men started pounding again.

Whoosh! The torches in the lounge brightened and Buddy Kool moved to the center of the room, holding a microphone. "Welcome to the Junga-Lounge!" he said. "The big show is ready to start! It will knock your socks off. It'll bring back memories — the prehistoric kind! Ha-ha!"

"Funny," Liz said. "Can we go now?"

Buddy Kool smiled at her. "Let me put it this way. NO!" He laughed. "You kids gotta

hang around for the big show." He pointed up.

Mike looked to the ceiling. "Huh? What do you mean hang — "

Fwing! Instantly a net dropped over the two kids and hoisted them up out of their chairs and upside down into the air.

"Whoa!" groaned Mike, flipping over. "Now I'm really glad I didn't eat anything!"

In a flash, the net was hanging right over the shark pool. It twisted two feet above the surface.

"Speaking of eating," Buddy Kool said, "how do you know a shark likes you?"

Liz and Mike glared at him.

"He comes back for seconds!"

CHOMP! The shark leaped up and snapped at Liz and Mike. It dived back and circled around.

"Get us out of here!" Liz demanded. "We're American kids and you can't do this to us!"

Boom-ba-boom-boom! Ba-boom-boom-ba!

"Oooh, too bad. The show's already starting," cooed Buddy Kool, sipping a frothy drink from a pineapple.

As the pounding got louder and faster, something totally amazing, unbelievable, and weird happened. The Mango Men suddenly stopped pounding. But the pounding went on!

Boom-ba-boom-boom! Ba-boom-boom-ba!

The sounds echoed up into the room. Up from below! The pounding came from under the floor! Under the ground! Under the Junga-Lounge!

Buddy Kool yelled into his microphone like a game show host. "Come on up! Join the party!"

As Liz fixed her eyes on the floor. Slowly, the floor began to slide open.

"Whoa!" yelled Mike, struggling to see. "Caves! Lots and lots of caves!"

"And lots and lots of Mango Men!" Liz cried.

Yes, beneath the floor, beneath the ground, were caves, hundreds of them, snaking down into the earth. And coming up through the caves were weedy men. They were dressed in suits made of twigs and grass and vines. They had sticks too.

"It's a whole underground world!" said Liz.

"Oh, the caves?" said Buddy, coiling his dangly hair curl so it hung just right. "They go way back. Way back. The caves have been there forever. It's where the Mango Men come from."

"And you too?" asked Liz.

"Me!" Buddy Kool laughed. "Nah, I come from New Jersey." Then he held the microphone away and leaned closer to Liz and Mike. "The truth is, the Mangoes got the sticks, I got the brains. But, they also got great big Tiki men."

Skkkssss! He slurped the last sip of juice from his pineapple. "You see, when I was a kid growing up, my friends always wanted to play baseball. I wanted to take over the world. This is a dream come true for me."

"Well, it's a nightmare for us," Liz growled.

Kool sighed. "I'll never forget the day when I fell through a hole and met the Mango Men. Boy, did I impress them! I could tell by the way they said, 'Ugh.' As they say, the rest is history. Or should I say, *prehistory*!"

Errr! Errr! The net swung lower and lower.

"You'll never get away with this!" Liz cried.

Buddy Kool frowned. "Hey, are you hungry?"

Mike's stomach growled. "Sure," he said. "But no curly fries. I don't — "

"Not you!" snapped Kool. "I was talking to the shark." He lowered Liz and Mike to the water. Then he stopped. "Wait, did I tell you the one about how you can tell a shark likes you?"

"Yes!" Mike snarled at him.

"Oh," Buddy Kool said. "Then I guess there's nothing more to say before I feed you to him!" He continued to lower the rope.

"No, wait! Tell us again!" cried Liz, watching the pool bubble below her.

"Yeah," Mike pleaded, "we liked it so much the first time! The punch line is great. We love it."

"Nah, you heard it already," said Buddy Kool. "It's spoiled."

"Oh, man!" went Mike.

Errrk! went the rope.

Splash! went the pool.

Snap! went the shark.

Zonerama!

KA — *RRRRRUNCH!*

No, it wasn't the shark. It was the door, bursting into splinters as three figures barreled into the lounge.

"Hey, that bamboo cost me a fortune!" yelled Buddy Kool, stopping the rope.

"Ha! We don't care about your door. We care about our friends!" Jeff shouted, gritting his teeth and swinging a bat over his head. Sean and Holly stepped up behind him.

Yes, the three best friends of Liz and Mike were standing in the doorway, fully equipped with baseballs, bats, and attitudes!

The Mango Men shook their thick wooden sticks. "Ugh! Ugh!" they chanted. Then they charged over the rope bridge at the three kids!

"Stand back!" snarled Sean. "Let's see what the grass guys can do against this!" He wound up and shot his fastball right at the men.

FWOOSH! The ball blazed through the lounge at top speed!

"Whoa!" gasped Mike. "The kid can throw!"

"Ugh!" cried the head Mango Man. He pushed his friends aside and swung with his thick wooden stick. *Whack!* The ball shot back at Jeff.

Jeff leaped over a mushroom table and — *fwap!* — caught the ball in his bare hand. "One out!"

And so the battle of the century began.

Bonk! Fapp! Thunk! Bwam! Sticks flailed, bats swung, baseballs hurtled, coconuts flew. Two Mango Men trapped Jeff against a mushroom table. Holly dived and swatted them with her bat.

Jeff leaped up free. "Thanks, Holly!"

"Hey, don't forget us!" Liz called out.

"Oh, right. The reason we're here!" Jeff said as he and Holly dodged a volley of pineapples, raced over to the net, jumped up, and clung to it. Then they started to swing the net back and forth.

The shark leaped up just as the net swung over the floor and Holly untied the rope.

WUMP! The sack of kids dropped to the floor.

CHOMP! The shark ate empty air.

Liz jumped up to see Buddy Kool slipping out the back door. At the same moment, a horde of Mango Men burst up from the caves below. "Ugh! Ugh!"

"Reinforcements!" Liz plucked some ripe nuts from overhead and heaved them. "Let's beat it!"

"Follow me!" yelled Sean. He led the

charge through a bunch of bustling bush boys. A bat in each hand, he and Holly spun their arms like twin propellers! *Whoosh-whoosh-whoosh!*

The Mango Men fell back for an instant and the five kids rushed through the bamboo door, and out the pitcher's mound to the field above.

"Yes! We're out!" cried Mike, jumping up and down. "We're saved!"

But what they saw next stopped them cold. The sun was falling behind the hills. Shadows fell over the jungly town.

The five giant Tiki heads had formed an enormous triangle around Grover's Mill. Their black eyes sparked and sizzled with eerie power.

"I knew it!" Liz cried. "We're too late!"

"Ha! Ha! And now — the grand finale!" Buddy Kool cried into a microphone from the top of the bleachers. "The end of Grover's Mill!"

The jungle went strangely calm and quiet. Shadows rose and fell from torches

held high by the huge army of Mango Men.

Liz knew something was about to happen. Something terrible.

Kool stood high on the bleachers. He held the stone tablet in front of him and translated the strange markings.

From the earth, dead men will rise
And grow the jungle with their eyes.
But what the great stone heads will steal
One past and future stone will heal.

"Oooh!" said Buddy Kool, putting the stone down. "Mysterious, huh? But that reminds me. What do you call a Tiki man who pops up from a baseball field in Grover's Mill? Give up? *Home!* Get it? *HOME!*" He buckled over in laughter.

Liz couldn't take it anymore. "Why you — " But before she could move an inch, the ground began to shake. Thunder exploded in the air. Lightning blasted across the sky. Then — *KKKK — ZZZZZ!*

The deep eyes of every giant Tiki man

glowed. Piercing red beams shot from one Tiki man to another until they formed a giant sizzling triangle around the town. It flashed like lightning.

"The triangle of weirdness," Liz gasped, unable to move. "Now, it's complete." Liz felt like giving up, but she knew it wasn't over. Something even worse was going to happen. But how? What could be worse than turning her town into a jungle?

Liz huddled next to her four friends. She listened to a distant sound. It was strange. It was weird.

Glub-glub!

"Is that . . . Lake Lake?" Mike mumbled.

It was Lake Lake. The giant O of water, sitting on the edge of town like milk at the bottom of a cereal bowl, was bubbling over!

Splooooosh! The water exploded in wave after enormous wave. It flooded out around the town.

"Grover's Mill is becoming an island!" cried Holly. "We're going back in time!"

Water roared across the dusty plains

surrounding Grover's Mill. Within minutes, the town was a tiny island in a vast gurgling sea.

"And now . . . for the really big finish!" Buddy Kool cried out from the top of the bleachers, snapping his fingers. "And, yes, folks, you may start your applause any time!"

Suddenly, from the big stone faces of the big stone heads, came deep, thundering sounds. The heads were talking. Talking . . . English!

"Revenge!" boomed the first head.

"Revenge!" boomed the second.

"Revenge! Revenge!" boomed the third and fourth heads.

"Let me guess," Liz snarled at the fifth head.

"Revenge!" it boomed, like the others.

"Maybe they only know one word," said Jeff.

"Too bad it's not a good word," Sean added.

"Yeah, they really have to work on that

vocabulary," Mike snapped. "Sean, give me one of your bats. I think I want to bonk some heads!"

Then, the five big Tiki heads in the triangle around Grover's Mill began to turn.

Scrape! Thump! Scrape! Scrape!

The five stone heads began to . . . walk!

Grover's Island

*S*crape! Thump! Scrape!

Liz and her friends stood stunned as the big heads scraped deep trenches in the earth. The ground shook. The air boiled from the hot red glow of the deep Tiki eyes.

All the people in Grover's Mill rushed around the kids. They looked afraid. "We need some answers!" someone in the crowd shouted. Liz looked into their faces. They were people she had known for a long time. She knew what they were feeling. She felt it, too. The sense of total doom.

Liz stepped forward. "The Tiki men are doing this with their weird powers," she told them. "They turned back time and brought the ancient jungle back. And now these Tiki heads want only one thing. To destroy us."

"Isn't that just a little *weird*?" someone asked.

"Yes!" Liz pleaded. "It's a lot weird! It's totally and absolutely weird! It's — "

ZZZZ — BLAM! A fiery red beam shot out of the Tiki men's eyes and exploded nearby.

"Yikes!" screamed Mike, gripping his bat tightly. "I think we get the message!"

"Run!" cried Mr. Duffey, snapping his bullwhip — *ka-fwap!* "Those mighty heads are up to no good! If one of them loses his balance, we'll be smushed!"

BLAM! BLAM! BLAM! All the heads fired at the crowd. The jungle lit up with the huge blasts.

"To the vines!" Mike shouted.

In a flash, the five kids ran along the jungle floor and leaped up. They each grabbed hold of a long vine hanging from the trees above.

Whoosh! From one vine to another, they swung in the trees, trying to stay ahead of the big heads.

ZZZZ — BLAM! A grove of palm trees burst apart near Jeff and Sean. The explosion sent them swinging off in another direction.

"Everybody meet on the hill!" yelled Holly swinging after them.

Liz swooped up into a tree and waited for Mike to catch up. He swung up next to her.

ZZZZ! The jungle lit up with the sizzling eyes of four Tiki men crashing swiftly after them.

"It's just you and me again, Mike," she said.

"Yeah, the odd team." He smiled. "But the big heads are getting closer, so maybe we should escape to play another day."

Liz nodded. "Watch out for head number five! He's hiding somewhere." She grabbed a vine and jumped.

"I'm right behind you!" yelled Mike, gripping his bat tightly in one hand and a vine in the other. He pushed off after Liz.

Whoosh! Swoop! Whoosh! Liz made her way from vine to vine. But as she swung down quickly to a dense clump of trees, a dark shape with bright eyes appeared among the branches.

"Uh-oh!" she cried. "I think I found *hiiiiiiim!*"

THWAPPPP!

"Ow!" Liz yelped. She smacked the dark shape hard, let go of her vine, and felt herself scraping down a rough, rocky surface.

"Help!" she screamed. "I'm on a Tiki man!"

THWAPPP!

"So am I!" yelped Mike, tumbling across the top of the same Tiki head.

"Mike, I'm slipping! I'm going to be crushed!" Liz shrieked, sliding down the giant nose toward the ground just as the giant head took a step.

In that instant, her foot caught on the Tiki's jutting chin. She clung fast to the tip of the nose and swung from it, looking up into its deep, dark, and very big nostrils.

"Whoa!" she cried. "Do Tiki heads sneeze?"

"I don't think so," Mike yelled down from above. "But then, they aren't supposed to walk or talk either!"

The Tiki head lowered its glowing eyes.

"Uh-oh! He's looking cross-eyed at me!" Liz shouted. "I think he's going to fire his eyes!"

"I never did like those eyes!" Mike sprawled flat on the head and extended his bat. Liz reached. Her fingers grasped the tip of the bat and Mike pulled up with all his strength just as the Tiki man's eyeballs flashed.

BLAM! The jungle ahead of them charred black instantly.

"I don't think he likes us up here!" Mike cried.

"Tough!" Liz snarled, reaching the top next to him. "Hey, I just thought of something. What's worse than a giraffe with a sore throat?"

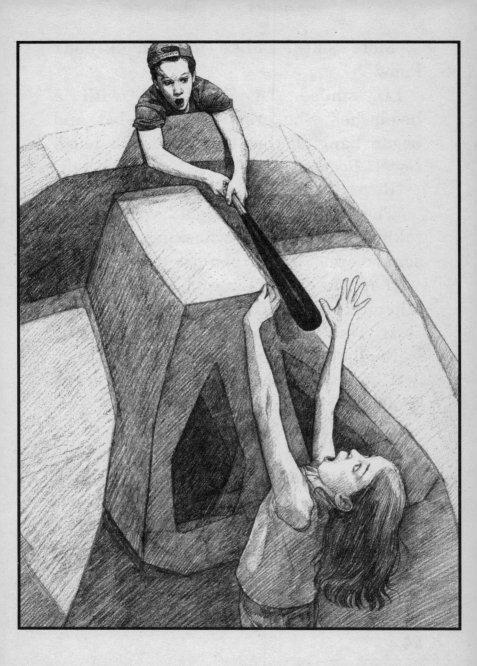

"More jokes?" Mike whined. "I don't know."

Liz smiled. "A Tiki head with a headache!" She grabbed Mike's bat and began banging the top of the Tiki head. *Boom! Boom!*

"Revenge!" thundered the Tiki man.

"That's the word, all right," yelled Mike, taking the bat and whacking the head some more. "And we can use it, too!"

That was when Liz and Mike saw the other Tiki heads. They were coming to help their Tiki head pal. And their eyeballs were all glowing and ready to fire.

"Uh-oh! Time to move along!" Liz cried. "Follow me!"

"Huh?" said Mike. "Follow you . . . where?"

But Liz grabbed his hand and took a running jump off the Tiki man's head, just as the other heads crowded around him.

They landed on one of the other Tiki heads.

"Revenge!" the head boomed.

They raced across that and jumped to another head. And from there to another and another.

"Revenge! Revenge!" boomed all the heads.

"Hey, just like stepping stones!" Mike shouted. "I love it!" But the Tiki heads didn't. They blasted at the kids with every leap.

BLAM! BLAM! BLAM! The jungle exploded with fiery flashes of incredible Tiki eyeball power. But the kids were too fast for them.

Leaping off the last head, Liz and Mike scrambled to the ground and ran as fast as their legs could carry them. They ran straight up the highest hill overlooking Grover's Mill and straight into the crowd of townspeople and their friends.

"They're coming!" Liz told everyone. "For their final attack!"

"And thanks to us, they're way mad," Mike added.

In the distance Buddy Kool was barking

commands into the microphone as his army of thousands of Mango Men massed for a huge assault.

The sun was setting quickly over Grover's Mill. Over what used to be their town.

Scrape! Thump! Scrape!
Boom-ba-boom-boom!

The sounds echoed up and around the hill from the jungle below. And then came those terrible quaking, thundering words again.

"Revenge! Revenge! Revenge! Revenge!"

The five friends huddled together.

"They're going to do that ray thing on us and zap us out of existence!" cried Holly.

"They'll take over once and for all!" Jeff said.

"We'll be the town that never was!" said Sean.

ZZZZ — *BLAM!* The Tiki men marched up the hill, blasting away with their deadly eyeballs, destroying everything in their path!

"I can't stand this!" Liz yelled out, jumping up. "If those Tiki men get here, we won't have any town left! We won't be living anywhere!"

Sean shook his head. "What would that be like?"

"It would be like . . . nothing!" shrieked Liz. She felt so angry she grabbed one of the baseball bats and slammed it on the ground next to her.

WHOOF! The ground crumbled away beneath her. Liz lost her balance and fell into a hole.

"Oh, not again!" she cried. "Man, I hate holes! What is with me today? I'm spending most of my time underground!" Then she looked around. "Hey, wait a second. There's something down here. A stone. And it's carved."

"Uh-oh," said Mike. "Tiki man number six?"

"No," she said. "I don't think so."

"Stand back!" yelled Mr. Duffey. "If it's stone and it's carved, it must be archaeological!"

He jumped down into the hole next to his daughter. "Golly, it's round," he announced.

"And flat," Liz added. "With a little hole in the middle like a wheel. It looks like — "

Mr. Duffey jumped up. "It's a millstone, used to mill or grind things. But . . . hmm . . . what would a millstone be doing here in Grover's Mill?"

"Uh . . . Dad?" Liz blinked. "Could this stone be, like, you know . . . the *Grover's Mill millstone*?"

Mr. Duffey gasped. "Daughter! You've done it! You've identified the most important artifact of our past! Yes! This *is* the Grover's Mill millstone! Too bad there's no more museum to display it."

THUMP! SCRAPE! THUMP! The stone Tiki men had nearly scraped and thumped their way to the top of the hill. The eyeballs readied themselves for a huge blast. Buddy Kool and his Mango Men were right behind them.

Liz was quiet for a while. She looked into the faces of all the townspeople around her. Then it hit her like a blast from a Tiki man's eyeballs! "That's what the stone tablet said! *But what the great stone heads will steal. . . .* That's Grover's Mill. *One past and future stone will heal.*"

"What's a *past and future stone*?" Sean asked.

Liz turned to the crowd. "This millstone!

It's our past, but it's also our future. The only chance we have against these heads is this stone. We need to dig it up. And then we need to — roll it!"

"Yes!" yelled Mike, jumping up and down. "Ka-pow! And down they go! It's brilliant, Liz. It's perfect! It's a plan!"

"I knew you'd do it!" Holly said.

"Liz is the smart one, everybody says so," Sean said, jumping into the hole with the others.

And in a flash, every grown-up and every child was digging away at the earth. Within minutes, the huge wheel-shaped stone was standing upright before them. And just in time.

ZZZZZ!

"The Tiki men!" cried Liz. "They're getting ready to blast us! We have to hurry!"

With Liz in the lead, the people of Grover's Mill moved the giant millstone to the crest of the hill. They aimed it, gave it a little push, and let it go!

RRRRRRR! The ground shook as the

round millstone rolled downhill. It picked up speed, thundering over rocks and mounds. With every bounce, it rolled faster. And faster. And faster!

It rolled right at the giant Tiki men. Their dark eyes flashed. It was almost as if they knew what was coming. But they just couldn't move fast enough.

KA — BOOOOOOOOOOOOOOOOM!

The famous Grover's Mill millstone slammed into them like a bowling ball into pins. The Tiki heads exploded into millions of tiny Tiki pebbles! The sky rained Tiki dust!

"Busted!" yelled Sean.

"Total gravel!" cried Holly.

"They're all broken up about this!" said Jeff.

"Major Tiki headache!" shouted Mike.

But the millstone kept rolling. Buddy Kool looked up at it. For the first time, it seemed as if he'd lost his cool. "Hey, people, wait! Can we talk? It's the Mango Men you want. All I do is tell a few jokes!"

The Mango Men didn't seem to like that. They raised their sticks. "Ugh!" they cried.

"Hey, I don't like your tone!" Buddy Kool took off down the hill. The Mango Men rushed after him.

But the stone kept rolling. It thundered across what used to be Main Street and rumbled to the ball field.

Buddy Kool dived below the pitcher's mound into his fancy Junga-Lounge. The Mango Men chased him into the caves below.

WHA — BOOOOM! The massive millstone crashed through the lounge's bamboo door, roared across the floor after them, tipped in the shark pool, and fell flat on its side.

Right over the cave entrance.

RMMM! It stopped there. The entrance was plugged. Buddy Kool and the Mango Men were trapped in the caves. Forever.

"Perfect shot!" Sean yelled from the hilltop.

"Yahoo!" whooped Mike, jumping up and down. "We did it!"

The revenge of the Tiki men had failed.

At that moment, the sounds of the jungle died down. All over town things went quiet and calm. A streak of light eased in from the east and the sky brightened.

It was morning.

That's when Liz and her friends noticed that something else was happening, too.

"Hey, the grass," Mike cried. "Look!"

Liz looked down to see the overgrown grass beneath their feet slither silently back into the earth. At once, the jungle trees, bushes, moss, and vines sank back into the ground where they had come from.

"My house!" shouted Principal Bell. "My green house! I see it!"

His house, all their houses.

And all the buildings and streets, cars and bikes, streetlights and telephone poles of Grover's Mill came back into view as the jungle slipped quietly away.

The waters receded and the desert

around town was dry again. Grover's Mill was not an island anymore. It was back to normal.

"To work!" boomed Principal Bell, forming his grass necklace into a bow tie. Miss Lieberman followed him down the hill. "School starts in just seventy-one-point-three days. Ah, math!"

Liz, Mike, Holly, Jeff, and Sean walked back to town and up Main Street together. Everyone was doing their usual stuff. Opening shops, eating at restaurants, buying groceries, having X rays.

Liz looked around. The town was messed up a little, especially her own house. But, everybody would help rebuild. You couldn't stop Grover's Mill that easily. No way.

"The whole thing is amazing," Holly muttered. "Almost as if it never happened."

"Weird is the word," said Liz. "But if there's one thing we learned, it's that Grover's Mill has been weird for a long time."

"Pretty much since the beginning," said Mike. "It'll probably stay that way, too."

Jeff tossed his baseball cap in the air. Sean caught it, laughed, and started to run with it.

Mike turned to Liz. "Looks like it's going to be nice today. What do you want to do?"

Liz smiled. "Why don't we just wait? I'm sure something will happen. After all — "

Bong! went the big donut clock, the sun shimmering off its glazed coating.

" — we do live in — "

Sssss! went the big pancake pan, a stream of smoke hissing into the golden air.

" — The Weird Zone!"

LITTLE  APPLE®

Here are some of our favorite Little Apples.

There are fun times ahead with kids just like you in Little Apple books! Once you take a bite out of a Little Apple—you'll want to read more!

Reading Excitement for Kids with BIG Appetites!

☐ NA45899-X **Amber Brown Is Not a Crayon**
Paula Danziger **$2.99**

☐ NA93425-2 **Amber Brown Goes Fourth**
Paula Danziger **$2.99**

☐ NA50207-7 **You Can't Eat Your Chicken Pox, Amber Brown**
Paula Danziger **$2.99**

☐ NA42833-0 **Catwings** Ursula K. LeGuin **$2.95**

☐ NA42832-2 **Catwings Return** Ursula K. LeGuin **$3.50**

☐ NA41821-1 **Class Clown** Johanna Hurwitz **$2.99**

☐ NA42400-9 **Five True Horse Stories**
Margaret Davidson **$2.99**

☐ NA43868-9 **The Haunting of Grade Three**
Grace Maccarone **$2.99**

☐ NA40966-2 **Rent a Third Grader** B.B. Hiller **$2.99**

☐ NA41944-7 **The Return of the Third Grade Ghost Hunters**
Grace Maccarone **$2.99**

☐ NA42031-3 **Teacher's Pet** Johanna Hurwitz **$3.50**

Available wherever you buy books...or use the coupon below.

- -

SCHOLASTIC INC., P.O. Box 7502, 2931 East McCarty Street, Jefferson City, MO 65102

Please send me the books I have checked above. I am enclosing $ _____ (please add $2.00 to cover shipping and handling). Send check or money order—no cash or C.O.D.s please.

Name_____

Address_____

City_____**State/Zip**_____

Please allow four to six weeks for delivery. Offer good in the U.S.A. only. Sorry, mail orders are not available to residents of Canada. Prices subject to change.   LA996